Leo and Ella are ordinary kids with an **EXTRAORDINARY** destiny!

Well, they're not really ordinary. Just read the first sentence of the book and you'll see.

They do, however, have an **EXTRAORDINARY** adventure in the **KINGDOM OF IZZAMBARD**.

Fancy a trip there?

You'd better hop on board!

Great Clarendon Street, Oxford OX2 6DP
Oxford University Press is a department of the University of Oxford.
It furthers the University's objective of excellence in research, scholarship,
and education by publishing worldwide in

Oxford New York

Auckland Cape Town Dar es Salaam Hong Kong Karachi
Kuala Lumpur Madrid Melbourne Mexico City Nairobi
New Delhi Shanghai Taipei Toronto

With offices in

Argentina Austria Brazil Chile Czech Republic France Greece
Guatemala Hungary Italy Japan Poland Portugal Singapore
South Korea Switzerland Thailand Turkey Ukraine Vietnam

First published 2016

British Library Cataloguing in Publication Data

Data available

ISBN: 978-0-19-274554-5

1 3 5 7 9 10 8 6 4 2

Printed in UK

Paper used in the production of this book is a natural,
recyclable product made from wood grown in sustainable forests
The manufacturing process conforms to the environmental
regulations of the country of origin

PICTURES BY Sam Usher

The Secret Railway

WENDY MEDDOUR

OXFORD
UNIVERSITY PRESS

TICKETS PLEASE!

WAIT! STOP RIGHT THERE!

Sorry, but you can't come on this journey until I've checked you're allowed on board. There's just one rule: you absolutely have to be a child. (Children *may* bring their own grown-up, but only if the grown-up promises to behave.) You'd be surprised just how many grown-ups try to sneak past the barrier on their own! That's why you have to answer the following questions. Please be as honest as you can. If any answer is **'YES'**, then you must **PUT THE BOOK DOWN AND WALK AWAY!!** But if all your answers are **'NO'**, then you may collect your ticket and continue—full steam ahead—into a world of mystery, magic, and adventure.

OK. Are you ready? Then concentrate, please:

QUESTION 1 Are you married?

QUESTION 2 Do you have any whiskers on your chin?

QUESTION 3 Do you worry about the size of your bottom?

QUESTION 4 Are you a member of the Women's Institute?

QUESTION 5 Have you ever bought a bungalow?

Are all your answers **NO?** Excellent. And thank goodness for that! You are **100% CHILD**. Here's your ticket:

You may now pass the barrier below.

DESTINATIONS

ALL ABOARD!

PLATFORM ONE

· THE STATION HOUSE ·

Ella and Leo Leggit were not ordinary children. 'Well, of course,' you'll say. 'No children are.' And you'd be right. I'm sure you're *very* peculiar. But what I mean is, Ella and Leo were *extremely* not ordinary. For example, Ella was the only eight-year-old girl in Biddleshire that could sing "Twinkle, Twinkle, Little Star", backwards. In French. Whilst sucking a lollipop. Upside down. And Leo was the only ten-year-old boy in Biddleshire that dreamt of being electricity every night. Great big swishing bolts of electricity lighting up the dark night sky. I know. The pair of them—not ordinary at all!

So when their parents, Mr and Mrs Leggit, bought an old station house at the edge of a forest near Little Higgleton, of course it wasn't going to be boring. It was going to be **AMAZING. INCREDIBLE. RIDICULOUS. FRIGHTENING. WONDERFUL. AND FULL OF ADVENTURE!** It's just that Leo and Ella didn't know that. Yet.

That's why they were sitting on cardboard boxes full of saucepans, sighing and missing their friends.

'The faces on you two could sink a battle ship!' Mrs Leggit said. 'Why don't you go and explore?'

'We've explored already.' Leo sighed deeply. 'Three empty bedrooms. One empty lounge. One empty office. And one empty kitchen.'

Ella nodded in agreement. 'And three empty toilets.'

'Mum doesn't mean explore the house,' Mr Leggit said, heaving a rubber plant through the hall. 'She means explore the great outdoors.'

'It's raining,' Ella complained.

'A bit of rain won't hurt you.' Mrs Leggit wrestled a kettle out of a box. 'You two should be having an adventure. Like we did in the old days. Go on. Off you go. Just make sure you're back in time for tea.'

Leo looked at the empty kitchen. 'What's for tea?'

'Cabbage,' Mrs Leggit replied.

'Mum, you *know* I hate cabbage.'

'Only joking.' Leo and Ella's mother grinned.

'I LOVE cabbage,' Ella said. 'And I love sprouts. And I love mushrooms.'

'Why do you have to love everything?' Leo asked, ruffling her hair.

Ella shrugged.

'Just make sure you're back by five o'clock,' Mrs Leggit said. 'And I'll just do some fish fingers, Leo.'

'I LOVE fish fi…'

Leo put his hand over Ella's mouth and tickled her until she wriggled like a trout. 'Dad, can me and Ella go and look in the workshop? The one behind the house. That's sort of "outdoors".'

'Don't see why not,' Mr Leggit said. 'As long as you're careful.'

'Oh! I LOVE workshops,' giggled Ella, getting free.

'You don't even know what workshops look like,' Leo said.

'Yes, I do,' Ella said back, even though she didn't really.

'Now remember,' Mr Leggit said. 'Back by five o'clock. And don't touch anything sharp!'

'We won't,' they yelled, as they slammed the station-house door.

PLATFORM TWO

· THE WORKSHOP ·

Now, I don't know if you've seen a lot of workshops. But the station workshop looked like all the rest. Red bricks. Tiny windows. A big wooden door. Not very impressive at all. But if you've read a lot of stories or been on a lot of adventures, you'll be aware that 'not very impressive things' always turn out to be the best! It's just that Leo and Ella didn't know that. Yet.

'Hurry up, Leo! Open the door,' Ella said, jumping up and down on the spot.

'I'm trying. It's just a bit stiff.'

'I can help,' Ella offered. 'I love helping.'

'No. I'm fine. And you're tiny.'

'I'm actually very normal-sized for eight.' Ella crossed her arms huffily.

Leo ignored her and pushed his shoulder against the heavy wooden door—but nothing happened.

Ella hummed a tune and twiddled her reddish-brown ponytail. Leo tried again. Nothing.

'Erm, actually Ella,' Leo said. But his sister didn't need to be asked. She threw the whole weight of her body against Leo's bottom very hard. He, in turn, pushed against the wood. Very hard. The door swung open and Leo and Ella tumbled right in!

'It's **HUGE**. And like a museum!' gasped Ella.

'More like a rubbish tip!' Leo said. 'No one's been in here for years!'

He was right. The station workshop was covered in cobwebs and dust. There were tables piled high with railway junk: tatty brown leather suitcases, funny-shaped parcels, odd metal lamps, whistles on string, curled up newspapers and forgotten coats spilling out of trunks labelled '**LOST**'. The floor was covered in curious bits and bobs too:

a rickety tea trolley, a stationmaster's hat, an iron spade, a golden birdcage, a dragon-shaped kite, and a bucket of coal.

'Oh look!' Ella exclaimed, clambering up onto one of the creaky old tables. 'It's a bright red HAT!'

'Get down!' Leo said.

But Ella wasn't listening. 'I've always wanted a bright red hat!' she said, climbing onto a suitcase. It wobbled as she leant forward and grabbed at the hat with both of her hands.

'You'll fall!' Leo cried, trying to steady the case.

'No, I won't.' Ella jumped back

down onto the ground. 'Isn't it lovely?'

'Ella,' Leo said, sternly. 'It's just a hat. And you could have hurt yourself.'

Ella grinned and stuck the bright red hat onto her head. It was too big and fell over her eyes. 'Do I look like an actress?' she asked.

'No. You look like a lampshade. And don't climb on the tables! It's dangerous.'

'But they're not sharp.' Ella spun round and knocked lots of papers on the floor.

'Ella! Careful!' shouted Leo. He reached down to pick them up. To be honest, he was feeling a bit nervous.

He couldn't quite explain why. But there was something about the workshop that made him feel strange. Sort of tingly. He tried to ignore it and blew the dust off the papers.

'Are they newspapers, Leo?' Ella asked. 'With news in?'

'No. Not newspapers. There aren't any words. They've just got lots of tiny numbers on.' Leo frowned. 'I think they're train timetables. You know. So that people know which train to catch and when.'

'Well that's just silly,' Ella said. 'There aren't any trains here at all!'

'They're old timetables,' Leo explained. 'And there used to be trains here. Just behind the workshop.

See. It even says: 1867. There. Right at the top.'

'Well, that's silly too,' Ella said.

'Why?' Leo asked.

'Because the timetables are new.' Ella pointed at some red circles that had been drawn around some of the times. 'See. It's even made my finger go red.'

'What? The ink's still wet!' Leo exclaimed. 'But how . . . I mean . . . that doesn't make sense.' Leo started to feel all tingly again.

But Ella wasn't listening. She'd already wandered off. 'Hey, Leo! I've found a funny mirror,' she said. 'It's got tiny birds all around the edge.' She held it up to her face.

She wanted to see her new hat. But it didn't work, so she put it back down on the table.

'It's not a mirror,' Leo said, going over and picking it up. 'It's a magnifying glass. And the birds on the top are griffins, I think.' The silver handle felt warm. Really warm. In fact, it made Leo's whole hand feel warm. He looked around at all the dust. No one else had been in the workshop for years. And Ella had only held it for a second. He couldn't understand it. The warm handle. The wet red ink. None of it made any sense.

'Leo. I've found another door.' Ella

shook a rusty padlock and began to fiddle with the lock.

'Leave it, Ella. It's only the back door of the workshop. There's only trees on the other side and . . .' Leo stopped. The magnifying glass had started to fizz! Only a tiny bit. Barely noticeable. But just enough so that he could feel it.

'Ella,' he said very slowly. 'There's something funny about this magnifying glass. It's fizzing.' He paused. 'I think it wants me to do something.'

'A mirror wants you to do something?! Mirrors don't normally do that!'

'I've told you. It's not a mirror,

Ella. It's a magnifying glass. It wants me to look at the train timetables. I don't know how I know but I know.'

Ella ran over to Leo, pushing the hat out of her eyes. 'Do it! Do it, Leo! Do what the mirror says.'

Leo looked at Ella. 'OK. I will.' Trembling slightly, he moved the griffin-trimmed magnifying glass above the tiny print on the timetable. That's when they both saw it! The red circles of ink began to swim across the page!

'The circles are moving!' Ella's eyes sparkled with excitement.

'I know,' Leo whispered. 'Don't move or they might stop!'

Ella didn't move. The circles continued to loop and swirl, and then, just as suddenly, they gathered around the time: 11:61.

'11:61,' Leo murmured.

'That's not actually a real time,' Ella said. 'I've learnt all about it at school.'

'Exactly,' Leo said. 'So what does it mean?'

'I don't know. Shall I sing you "Twinkle, Twinkle, Little Star" backwards—and in French? I'm much better at singing than "time".'

'Maybe later,' Leo said, peering through the magnifying glass again. 'Time. Time. Time. Time,' he muttered, looking around the cluttered workshop for clues. 'Oh! I've got it! Look! Look at that big clock on the wall!'

'What about it?' asked Ella. 'It's just a clock.'

'No. It's not. Just look at the time.'

Ella looked.

'See?' Leo said.

'Almost. I think.' Ella fiddled with her hair. She really hated 'time'. All those 'little' and 'big' hands muddled her up.

'The numbers are wrong,' Leo explained. 'There should only be 60 minutes in an hour. But that clock thinks there are 65!' Leo was right. The minute hand was pointing to 61. In fact, the hands were pointing to 11.61!

Leo looked at Ella. Then, he looked at the timetable. Then, he looked at the padlock on the door.

'Are you thinking what I'm thinking?' Leo asked.

'I don't know,' Ella said. 'Are you thinking that you'd like to borrow my hat? Because, the thing is, even though I like you, I don't really want to share it.'

'NO!' Leo said. 'I am thinking that 11.61 might be the code for the rusty padlock, you banana!'

'Oh yes!' Ella grinned. Leo was such a clever big brother. And it was great that he didn't like hats. 'Let's try!'

They both squeezed their way between the dusty tables and ran to the padlocked door.

'OK,' Leo said. 'Here goes. But

don't get too excited—because there's only going to be a wood on the other side.'

'I'm quite excited anyway.' Ella stroked the feathers on her hat. 'I can't help it. I LOVE IT when we work things out!'

'I know.' Leo smiled. Then, still holding the slightly fizzing magnifying glass in one hand, he twiddled the combination lock and put in the numbers:

11:61

PING! The rusty lock sprang open. And so did the workshop's back door!

'B ….b…but, that wasn't supposed to really work!' Leo stammered.

'Leo, look!' Ella exclaimed. 'It's not

just trees. 'It's a . . . it's a . . . a railway station!'

And true enough, it was. Stretching out before them was an enormous, old-fashioned railway platform all covered in strangely glowing honeysuckle and vines!

'I don't like this,' Leo said. 'I don't like this at all. Something's wrong. This can't be a railway station. There isn't a railway station behind our house. Come on, Ella. Quick! Let's go home.'

'No thank you!' Ella squawked. 'I LOVE railway stations. And I promise I won't touch anything sharp!'

Before Leo could put out an arm to stop her, Ella had jammed her big red hat firmly onto her head and run through the open door!

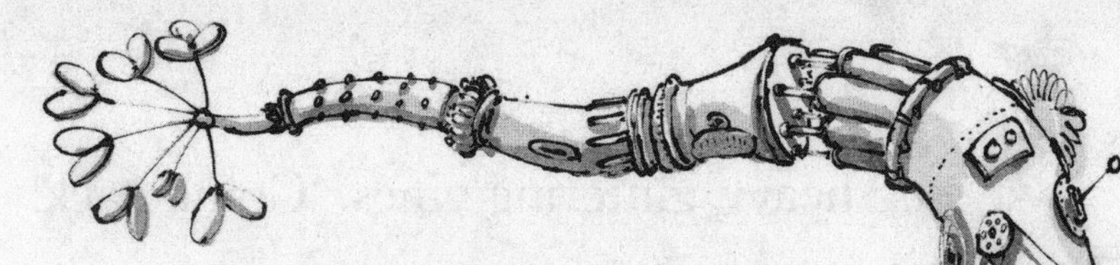

PLATFORM THREE

·TOO MUCH SUGAR·

Leo did NOT want to chase after his little sister. In fact, it was the last thing he wanted to do. He thought that railway platforms that *shouldn't* be there were best avoided. He wanted to shut the door, walk away, and go home. But he was a big brother. And unfortunately, as we all know, big brothers *can't* just walk away.

'Ella!' he cried, pushing through

the heavy, glittering vines. 'Come back! Wait for me!'

BANG. The door slammed shut behind him as his footsteps echoed on the stone.

'Everything's magic, Leo!' Ella was spinning around again. 'It's all twinkly and sparkly and bright.'

'No. It's not magic, Ella,' Leo said, catching up with her. He stopped and put on his best 'grown-up' voice: 'Actually, it's not even here. It's just in our imaginations. The whole thing. The railway. The platform. The glittery plants. We've probably just had too much sugar.'

'Too much sugar?!' Ella stopped spinning as her hat fell off. 'I've not even had a biscuit today.'

'Then we must be overexcited.'

'Overexcited?' Ella frowned.

'Yes . . . because of the move.'

Ella giggled. 'You sound just like Mum!'

'I do not.' Leo grabbed her by the hand. 'I'm just saying that there isn't a railway platform behind our house so none of this can be real. It's just in our imaginations.'

'But I don't have a train station in my imagination,' Ella said. 'I have pink sheep and trees made out of chocolate and . . . ouch . . . you're hurting my hand.'

'I just want to get us back home,' Leo said, pushing a scratchy, hard vine out of his face.

'But I like it here. And Mum and Dad sold our home.'

'I mean the new one, silly,' Leo said. He dragged Ella back down the platform and tried to open the door.

'What's the matter?' Ella asked.

'There isn't a handle! How am I meant to open a door without a handle?!'

'Just push,' Ella said. Leo pushed. The door didn't move.

'Now look what you've done!' Leo said.

'What have I done?' Ella asked.

'You've got us stuck!'

'Where?'

'On a railway platform, you banana!'

'But you said it wasn't here.'

'Of course it's here.' Leo stamped his feet on the glittery platform.

Ella's bottom lip started to wobble. 'You are not making sense,' she said. 'I don't like it when you don't make sense. And I don't like it when you get cross.'

'I'm not cross,' Leo said, softening and putting his arm around her little shoulder. 'I'm just . . .'

'Just what?' sniffed Ella.

'I'm just . . . feeling a bit stuck and unsure.'

Ella was confused. Big brothers

aren't supposed to feel stuck and unsure.

HUMMMMMMMMMMMMMMMM

'Oh, please don't start singing, Ella!' Leo said. 'If you start singing "Twinkle, Twinkle, Little Star" backwards, I'm going to . . . '

'I'm not singing,' Ella said.

HUMMMMMMMMMMMMMMMM

'Yes, you are!'

'No, I'm not,' Ella said. 'Your pocket is humming. That's all.'

Leo looked at his pocket as if it didn't belong to him. 'That's all! That's all! My pocket is humming, that's ALL!!'

'Yes,' Ella said. 'Are you getting cross again?'

'No. I'm not getting cross. I just don't

like it when pockets hum! Pockets are not supposed to *hum*. Railway stations are not supposed to *appear.* I don't understand it. And I don't like what I don't understand!'

'Of course you understand it,' Ella said. 'It's just an imaginary mirror humming in your imaginary pocket. Take it out and see what it wants.'

'It's a *magnifying glass*, not a mirror!' Leo said. 'And my pocket's not imaginary.'

'It might be if you've had too much sugar.'

'Ella!' Leo exclaimed. Then, because he didn't really have a choice, he took the humming magnifying glass out. It fizzed and the silver griffins seemed to sparkle ever brighter.

'How am I supposed to know what it wants?'

'Easy peasy,' Ella said.

'What?'

'Easy peasy. It just wants us to get on the puffetty train.'

'What puffetty train?!' asked Leo, nervously.

CHOOOOOOO CHOOOOOOOOO!

'That one.' Ella pointed at a big bellowing puff of steam, and the train engine hissing its way through it!

PLATFORM FOUR

· BUCKLES AND BUTTERFLIES ·

'THE TRAIN NOW ARRIVING AT PLATFORM ONE IS THE 11:61 IZZAMBARD EXPRESS,' boomed a voice.

Leo jumped. The voice seemed to come from everywhere. The sky. The vines. Even the railway tracks.

'Who said that?!' Leo asked.

'Our imaginations,' Ella said. 'Look! Look at the train!' And there it was: the most magnificent, shining, purple and gold engine, coming out of the steam like a dragon.

Leo couldn't help himself. He gasped with delight. Ella jumped up and down excitedly. 'Stop! Train! Please! Stop!!'

CHOOOOOOOOOOOOOOOOOOOOO

There was a big splurge of steam as brakes screeched and the train came to a halt. The doors opened but nobody got off. Nobody got on. Leo and Ella looked at each other and wondered what to do.

HUMMMMMMMMMMMMMMMMM

'Leo,' Ella said. 'Your mirror is humming again.'

'It's a magnifying glass,' Leo corrected.

'Well, I think it's trying to tell us to get on,' Ella said.

'Well, I think it's trying to tell us NOT to!' Leo said.

HUMMMMMMMMMMMMMMMM

'THE TRAIN AT PLATFORM ONE WILL BE LEAVING THE STATION ANY SECOND NOW AND IT DEFINITELY WON'T BE LATE,' boomed the voice. But this time, it wasn't coming from everywhere. It was coming from somewhere. In fact, it was definitely coming from inside the carriage. Suddenly, a man's face appeared at the window!

'Arghhhh!' Ella leapt backwards.

'ARGHHHHHHHHH!' screamed

the man, disappearing back into the carriage.

Leo and Ella looked at each other. They edged their way towards the carriage. From behind a velvet seat, a little voice whimpered:

'T . . . t . . . tell G . . . G . . . Griselda, I'm trying my b . . . b . . . best to be on time, but it's hard to get it right when the c . . . c . . . clock doesn't work. And also t . . . t . . . tell her, I haven't been feeling myself lately. I'm probably coming down with something. And . . .' The face peered out from behind the seat. 'Oh. You don't look very clockwork.'

'Pardon?' Leo said.

'Sorry. I'm sure you are clockwork. G…G…Griselda's so brilliant at making you all. It's just that . . . Forgive me. Am I late? Please don't tell G . . . G . . . Griselda if I'm late.'

'We are most certainly NOT made of clockwork,' Leo said.

'What? You mean you're real!' the man said, peeping out again.

'No,' Ella said. 'We're just in your

imagination. Especially if you've had too much sugar.'

'Ssshh, Ella,' Leo said. 'You'll confuse him.'

'Are you quite sure you're not clockwork?' asked the man.

'Of course we're sure,' Leo replied.

'Well, goodness me! So you're definitely not one of G . . . G . . . Griselda's spies?'

'Who's G . . . G . . .Griselda?' asked Ella. 'And why are you hiding behind the seat? Grown ups aren't meant to do that.'

'"Who's Griselda"? You mean you don't know?'

'Nope. Never even heard of her,' Leo said.

'Well, blow me down and call me a unicorn!' said the man, coming out from his hiding place and standing up. He was taller than Leo had expected him to be and more handsome than Ella had expected him to be. The buttons on his turquoise uniform shone and made them both blink.

'I'm Bartholomew Buckle,' he said. 'Pleasure to meet you.' Then, without warning, he leapt forward and pinched Leo's arm.

'OUCH!' Leo yelped. 'Why did you do that?'

Bartholomew Buckle chuckled. 'You really aren't clockwork! Well, I never thought I'd see the day! Two Warm Hearts. Here on Platform One. You must be from the Other World!' Bartholomew Buckle's face changed. 'You'd better jump in. Otherwise, something awful will happen. Something terrible. Something dreadful. Something . . .' Bartholomew collapsed onto the seat and dabbed his forehead with his handkerchief.

'Are you all right?' Ella asked, quickly grabbing her hat.

'Oh. Don't you worry about me.

I always get faint when I'm running out of time.' Bartholomew wiped his forehead with his hankie again.

Ella sat next to him. 'My name is Ella. Do you like my hat?'

'I do,' said Bartholomew. 'Please. Just call me Barty.'

'Get off the train,' Leo snapped, grabbing Ella's hand. 'Don't talk to him. We're not going anywhere. Especially not with someone that pinches people!'

Barty leapt to his feet. 'Oh, but you must! It's not safe for you here!' His eyes were wide and filled with fear. 'I can't wait at the platform much longer. If . . . if . . . the train is late to its next destination, even once, she'll never release me. I'll be stuck on this train for ever. And . . . '

HUMMMMMMMMMMMMMMMMM

Leo had forgotten all about the magnifying glass.

HUMMMMMMMMMMMMMMMMM

It was getting louder. 'Be quiet!' Leo said, pulling it out of his pocket.

'Wait a minute? Is that? Is . . . Is that?' Barty stammered.

'It's a mirror,' Ella said, proudly.

'For the last time, it is NOT a mirror!' Leo said. 'It's just a silly old, noisy, stupid magnifying glass.'

Barty looked like he'd seen a ghost. 'It's not just a "silly old, noisy, stupid magnifying glass!"' he said. 'It's one of the ANCIENT MAGICAL

OBJECTS from the Kingdom of Izzambard!'

Before Leo could ask what Barty meant, an ENORMOUS vine leaf burst through the window into the train.

'Arghhhh!' screamed Ella.

'Keep still!' Leo shouted, jumping to her rescue. He pulled the twisting vine off his sister's hat. It was hard. Hard as steel.

'Oh no! We're running late!' cried Barty, disappearing into the next carriage. 'G . . . G . . . Griselda's clockwork vines will suffocate us all!'

The engines started to chug and hiss as the train began to move:

'THIS TRAIN HAS ALREADY LEFT PLATFORM ONE!!' boomed a voice.

Leo pulled the sparkling steel vine out of the window and threw it onto the track. It CLATTERED and CRASHED. Then, he ran back to Ella to check that she wasn't hurt.

'I'm not scratched. But I don't think I like G . . . G . . . Griselda,' Ella said. 'Leo. Can we go home?' Leo nodded. 'STOP THE TRAIN!' he shouted.

'Stop the train? Home? Oh dear,' Barty said, running back into the carriage and dabbing his head with his handkerchief. 'You can't leave, my little Warm Hearts. And you can't go back.' He leant out of the window to check that the vines had gone.

'Why not?' Leo demanded. The magnifying glass hummed.

'Because you've got one of Izzambard's ancient magical objects, so you must return it to its rightful owner.'

HUMMMMMMM went the magnifying glass.

CHOOOOOOO CHOOOOOOO went the train.

'But we don't even know who that is!' Leo said.

'The Chief Snarkarian at the Great Grand Library of Snarks,' Barty said.

Leo looked out of the window. The train was moving fast. Too fast to jump. 'And if we don't?' he said.

Barty wiped his forehead with his hankie: 'And if you don't . . . ' he paused.

'What?' asked Ella.

'Well, the thing is, oh dear, you see, if you don't . . . '

'WHAT?' Leo shouted.

'Well, if you don't, then your door to the Other World will NEVER, EVER open again!'

News like that is never easy to hear. Leo couldn't bear the thought of NEVER snuggling up in his Other World bed and dreaming of being electricity ever again! But something had caught Ella's attention. It was the steam. Or rather, it wasn't the steam. It was something inside the steam.

'Leo! Look! Look! The steam is full of tiny blue butterflies!'

Leo hadn't got time for butterflies. He hadn't got time for steam. There must be a way to get back home. Maybe Barty was wrong. Maybe Barty was . . . Hang on a minute. Where was Barty?

'He's gone!' Leo said, looking behind the seats and under the tables.

'Ooh. One's landed on my nose,' Ella said. 'It's all clinketty and metal all close up! It's made of bits. Just like a watch!' She blew the delicate clockwork butterfly out from underneath the brim of her hat.

'I don't care about butterflies, Ella. I don't care about bits. I just want to see Barty Buckle. NOW!'

'Barty Buckle. Butterflies. Bits.'

Ella had forgotten all about Griselda's vines. 'They all begin with the letter B. B is my favourite letter. What's your favourite letter, Leo?'

'It doesn't matter,' snapped Leo, grabbing Ella's hand and charging down the middle of the railway compartments.

Barty was right at the end of the train. But he wasn't alone. He was holding a lever behind two squirrels. And the squirrels were shovelling coal into the engine as fast as they could!

'Wow!' Ella said. 'My imagination is really good! I can see squirrels. And they're wearing pretty waistcoats!'

Leo closed his eyes. Then he opened them. The squirrels in waistcoats were still there. It was all too strange.

'BARTHOLOMEW BUCKLE!' Leo shouted, above the **CHUFF** and the **HISS** of the engine. 'I ORDER YOU TO STOP THIS TRAIN! WE DON'T WANT TO GO TO THE GREAT GRAND LIBRARY OF SNARKS AND WE NEED TO GET BACK TO THE OTHER WORLD NOW!'

The squirrels both stopped shovelling, their tails twitching nervously.

'Apologies, Lord and Lady Asquith,' Barty said. 'Please don't be alarmed. The little Warm Hearts mean no harm. Do carry on shovelling. You know what will happen if we're late.' The squirrels nodded and started shovelling twice as fast.

'BARTHO—' Leo broke off, as Barty ran over and put his finger on his lips.

'Please don't raise your voice. You'll scare Lord and Lady Asquith. And then, where will we be?' Barty looked at his watch. 'Oh dear. It's stopped again. Never mind. Let's go and talk nicely in the carriage.'

Barty lifted his cap, wiped his

hankie on his brow, and wandered down the corridor. Ella curtsied at the squirrels and chased after him.

Leo didn't want to talk nicely in the carriage. Leo didn't want to talk nicely anywhere. But he had no choice. With his head sunk into his chest and a softly humming magnifying glass hanging at his side, he followed Barty and Ella down the empty train and joined them around an oak table-top.

'Right,' Barty said, jumping on the table. 'Come on. Quick. Follow me.'

'Follow you where?' Ella asked.

'Follow me into The Past, of course,' Barty said. 'Well, not The Past, exactly, but the place where we can look at it. Why do you think we made the tables out of oak? It's one of the oldest woods. Remembers The Past far better than the others.'

And with that, Barty jumped into the table as if it was the sea. There. Splash. Vanished!

Ella gasped. 'He's gone!' She rubbed the oak with her fingertips. 'He's gone! Right through the table!'

Leo's mouth had gone dry. 'Well, don't go and . . . ' But it was too late. Ella had already clambered on top of the table and jumped inside.

Leo groaned. Some metal butterflies tinkled around his face. He closed his eyes and thought hard:

QUESTION: What do you do if your little sister jumps through a table top?

ANSWER: Jump straight after her. That's what big brothers do.

And so he did.

PLATFORM SIX

· TABLE TOPS AND TIME WADERS ·

It was the strangest feeling. Leo couldn't quite describe it. It didn't feel the same as being electricity. More like being a feather, floating downwards, in an enormous empty wooden fish bowl. (I know. Sorry. But I did say it was hard to describe.)

'This is amazing,' Ella yelled, holding her hat tight and swirling through the air.

Leo was heavier than Ella so soon caught her up. He grabbed her hand, and they spun like two sycamore leaves. Or two spinning fish. Or maybe just two feathers. Yes. That would be right. Meanwhile, Barty was waiting at the bottom of the bowl, cross-legged, and shaking his watch.

'You two took your time. But fortunately, time stops in here. Griselda has no power over the past. So I suppose it doesn't really matter. In fact, I suppose I can wait all day.'

Leo and Ella landed softly on the oak floor. Surprisingly, it didn't hurt at all. The floor was polished and slippery—just like the table top on the train. This made it rather difficult to stand up. Leo and Ella started to slip about as if they were ice-skating.

'Pop these Time Waders on,' Barty said, throwing them some special sort of shoes. 'And you'll need your Past Prisms, too.' He handed them each a pair of emerald-framed glasses.

Ella put her glasses on, then took off her pumps and wriggled her toes into her Time Waders. They sucked to the floor like those fish that clean the tank.

Leo tried not to show it, but he loved his Time Waders. He was desperate to try walking up the wall!

'Concentrate please,' Barty said. 'The Past is about to start. Just sit down on the Time Told cushions if you want a good view.'

Ella and Leo weren't sure where to go, but the Time Waders seemed to guide them to exactly the right spot. They collapsed onto the softly padded chairs and Leo put the magnifying glass in his pocket.

'Did you say that The Past was about to start?' Ella asked.

'That's right,' Barty said. 'If you don't know The Past, how can you know The Present?'

The enormous wooden goldfish bowl (for how else could it be described?) went completely dark. Then, one side of the bowl lit up and some blue butterflies flickered across the screen.

'Ooh. It's like a cinema,' Ella said, fiddling with her Past Prisms. 'Can we have some popcorn?'

'Some popwhat? No. Just watch,' Barty said. 'There's a lot you need to learn.'

A deep oak voice began to thunder in the darkness. (If you haven't heard oak speak before, don't worry. It sounds exactly like you think it probably would.)

'Once Upon a Time, the Kingdom of Izzambard was the envy of the Secret World. The silver mists of magic glistened in its woods: they spilled across its mountains and streams.'

Leo and Ella watched in amazement as the screen filled with images of unicorns, golden birds and flickering fish with crystal-topped wings. They saw courts full of dancing and laughter—fairies, elves, pixies and sprites and royalty in magnificent gowns.

The oak voice became even deeper:

'But then, the Queen was gone and the Quiet Days began. Very slowly, the clocks in Izzambard became more brilliant, but all eyes were too tear-filled to notice.

'All eyes except for King Buckle's. Even in his grief he noticed the clocks' beauty and had an idea as to how he might mend his son's broken heart. For it had been a year since the kingdom's young Prince had smiled. That's why King Buckle broke the Secrecy Laws and sought out the Grand Master of the Clockmakers. That's why he sent a convoy of griffins to the Time-Ticker's Palace to ask the Grand Master Clockmaker to fix his son, even though this was forbidden.'

Ella was on the edge of her Time Told Cushion. This was better than any film she'd ever seen! 'He looks a bit like you,' she said, pointing to the young Prince on the screen.

'Shhhh,' Barty said. 'Listen.'

PLATFORM SEVEN

· A CLOCKMAKER ON A · MOONBEAM

'The griffins should never have entered the Time-Ticker's Palace or set eyes upon the Grand Master Clockmaker. King Buckle should never have broken the Kingdom's first rules. But he invited the Clockmaker to court to fix his son. No one expected what happened next. The Clockmaker was neither old nor crooked. She arrived on a moonbeam astride a silver unicorn. She wore a trailing gown of white crystal and black lace. The court was bewitched.'

Leo sighed in wonder as the figure glided across the screen.

'The Clockmaker's name was Griselda. The Old Queen's name was forgotten. The King ordered Izzambard's architects to build a white alabaster workshop in the palace grounds and the Clockmaker set to work. Soon, the halls of Izzambard were filled with wonders: metal-tipped butterflies, mysterious musical boxes, mechanical insects, flowers, and birds. And when Griselda fixed the Prince, she became Izzambard's new Queen.'

'Wow! She is lovely!' Ella said, gazing at The Past as it flashed in front of them, Griselda's black and white dress twirling in the rose gardens of the court.

'Lovely,' Leo repeated, in a daze.

'G . . .G . . . G . . . Griselda is not LOVELY!' shrieked Barty. 'She is EVIL.'

'How did she fix the Prince?' Leo asked, snapping out of his trance.

'By giving him a gift,' Barty replied. 'An incredible gift of—'

'Slowly, all of the Kingdom's magic was banished.' The oak voice had begun again. *'Queen Griselda ruled the land with a clockwork heart of steel. With the Old Queen gone, and the King powerless in her control, she entrapped the Prince on board a train. Only if all the ancient magical objects are found and restored to their rightful owners, will the magic of Izzambard ever return.'*

Suddenly, the screen went dark. The voice had gone. Ella and Leo blinked and took off their Past Prisms. The soft light returned.

Ella stared at Barty. Then she jumped up and curtsied: 'You're a prince,' she said. 'An actual prince.'

'You're the one that wouldn't smile,' Leo said.

Barty nodded. 'Now you know The Past, you must help me fix The Present. You must return the Snarkifying Glass to the Chief Snarkarian at the Great Grand Library of Snarks.'

HUMMMMMMMM hummed the Snarkifying Glass, excitedly.

'Hang on!' Leo said. 'We haven't agreed to return it yet!'

HUMMMMMMMMMMMMMMMMM

Ella glared at Leo. It was the face that said: 'Don't let me down.' Leo hated it when Ella did that face.

'Oh. All right,' Leo said. 'Get us out of this oak table and I'll think about it.' (Which was probably one of the strangest sentences he'd ever said.) He pulled off his Time Waders and put his trainers back on. Ella did the same. Without even saying goodbye the Time Waders slurped across the floor and disappeared!

'OK. I'll take you back to The Present,' Barty said. 'Just click your fingers and shout "RETURN".'

Leo didn't wait to be told twice. He grabbed Ella's hand and shouted: 'RETURN! PLEASE! NOW!'

PLATFORM EIGHT

· THE INCREDIBLE GIFT ·

Ella, Leo, and Barty tumbled out of the table-top back into their seats on the train. (You may find that difficult to believe. But then, so did Leo.) He was still knocking the solid oak with his knuckles when something squeaked:

'Refreshments? We've got elderflower fuzzle, graspberry drops, flipjacks and whizzle-ade.'

Ella and Leo both gasped.

'Don't be alarmed.' Barty smiled. 'It's only Cogg. Three whizzle-ades with straws, please. I'm always thirsty after going to see The Past.' A butterfly fluttered onto his cap.

'Uh-oh. Don't speak,' Barty warned, brushing it away. 'It's one of Griselda's mechanical spies. They may have heard too much already.'

They watched as the butterfly flew off.

'Right then, Prince Buckle,' Cogg said. 'Three whizzle-ades, coming right up.'

Leo felt dizzy. Squirrel-powered trains. Clockwork vines. Butterfly spies. Time Waders. Beautiful, evil

Grand Master Clockmakers. Jump-through table-tops. And now this. A . . . a . . . a . . . well, it's not easy to describe a Cogg to a Warm Heart. (I'm guessing you're a Warm Heart too?) But I'll try . . .

Cogg was probably one of the most complicated designs that the Evil Clockmaker had ever made. No one had thought it even possible. Part clockwork. Part Warm Heart. Think of an alarm clock with a spirit. Of course, Cogg didn't look like an alarm clock. Not on the outside, anyway. No. He looked like an extremely large vacuum cleaner on wheels. You know. The sort that can talk and that have extendable arms.

Only he was made of copper, not plastic. And he had a retractable sun-roof, in case it rained on his parts.

Ella was now grinning (because she was only eight). But Leo was too shocked to speak.

'Are you a spy?' Ella asked. 'Like the butterflies?'

Cogg's middle section started to whizz round and flash. 'Don't say things like that. You'll make me malfunction!'

'Of course he's not a spy,' Barty said. 'He's my best friend.' The Prince smiled.

Smiled. Ella remembered what the oak voice had said. Griselda had 'fixed' the Prince by giving him a gift that made him smile again. It must have been Cogg!

'You're the Prince's present, aren't you?'

Cogg made a very funny noise. A sort of 'WIBBBLLLEEEHOOOOKERPAH'. It may have been a laugh. But it's hard to tell when you're not familiar with talking vacuum cleaner sounds.

Ella giggled.

Leo sucked hard on his straw. (The whizzle-ade was the best thing he'd ever tasted, but it's annoying when your little sister works things out first.) 'Whoever you two are,' he said, 'let's just return this stupid Snarkifying Glass and go home.'

'Shhhh,' said Barty, pointing to a

butterfly that had landed on Ella's hat. 'Cogg! Debutterfly her!'

Cogg swizzled a nozzle towards Ella's hat and blew out a stream of blue air. The butterfly clattered onto the table then flew away.

'Debutterflying complete,' Cogg said.

'Will it be all right?!' Ella asked. (She LOVED butterflies.)

'Oh yes, its memory will be empty, that's all.'

'Wow!' Ella moved away from the fading blue smoke. 'Can we take some of that forgetting smoke home? Our parents are going to be furious when we get back to the Other World.'

Leo nodded. 'You're right. Better to make them forget. They'll have been worried sick.'

'No they won't,' Barty said. 'No one will be missing you.'

'Yes they will,' Ella insisted. 'Lots of people like us in the Other World.'

'I'm sure that's true.' Barty dabbed

at his forehead. 'But time stops in the Other World when you come into this one, so no one will have noticed you've gone.'

'Oh, that's good.' Ella adjusted her hat.

'What? No! It's not good,' Leo shrieked. 'Not good at all! If time stops in our world when we come into this one, then we could be stuck on this train for ever AND NO ONE WOULD EVEN NOTICE!'

PLATFORM NINE

· THE EVIL CLOCKMAKER ·

When you're a boy that dreams that he's electricity every night, it's not easy being stuck on a squirrel-powered train, with a humming magnifying glass, a talking vacuum cleaner, and a prince telling you that you can't go home. Leo was not feeling like electricity. He was feeling like a soggy little match. And he didn't like feeling like a soggy match.

In fact, he was finding it very hard. Cogg sensed something was wrong, so began to vacuum Leo's back. But Leo didn't like being vacuumed. He wasn't used to it.

'Go away!' Leo snapped.

Cogg made a strange deflating noise but Barty didn't notice. In fact, he just jumped up and ran out of the carriage.

'Now where's he gone?' Leo asked.

Suddenly, a voice boomed out: 'WE WILL SHORTLY BE ARRIVING AT SNARKSVILLE STATION. PLEASE BE CAREFUL WHEN ALIGHTING FROM THE TRAIN AND MAKE SURE YOU HAVE ALL YOUR

LUGGAGE WITH YOU.'

'Who's he talking to?' Ella asked. 'We're the only ones on the train.'

Cogg made a peculiar whizzing noise. A sort of **KEZZZRRRRRRR**. (It was the noise Cogg made whenever he didn't want to tell the truth. But Ella and Leo didn't know that. Yet. And I'm afraid I can't explain 'the truth', in case a passing butterfly overhears.)

Barty rushed back into the carriage, tapping his watch. 'Thank goodness we're not late! At least, I think we're not late. G . . . G . . . Griselda plays about with time, so we never really know. But the clockwork vines haven't started to creep. So I think we're fine!'

There was a gush of steam and butterflies, and the train came to a halt. The platform was empty. And it didn't look like the one near the workshop. It wasn't all silver coated and glittery. It looked like it was made out of paper! And when the carriage doors sprang open, it smelt of a mixture of books and museums and lavender.

'Why does it smell of lavender?' Ella asked.

'It helps you go to sleep at bedtime,' Cogg replied, as if that made any sense.

'Now,' Barty said, 'Listen carefully. 'You must return the Snarkifying Glass to the Great Grand Snarkarian Petunia Olive. She will then give you the Sleeping Key. Bring the key back to the train and I'll promise to get you home. But don't be late. You know I can't wait for long. If the train's late, I'll be stuck on it for ever.'

'How will we know if we're late?' Ella asked.

Barty flicked his watch. The long hand was twitching jerkily. 'You won't,' he replied. 'But if time speeds up, hurry on back. Or you'll get trapped by Griselda's vines!'

'How will we find the Great Grand Library of Snarks?' Leo demanded.

'I'll show you!' Cogg blurted out. 'Let me go. Please!'

HUMMMMMMMMMM hummed the Snarkifying Glass.

'All right,' Barty said. 'But be careful! And be quick! There's no time to lose. Or rather, there might be. But, anyway. You know what I mean!'

'Don't worry. We'll be straight back,' Leo said. He grabbed his sister's hand. OK. So he was chasing a talking vacuum cleaner. And OK, he was looking for a Great Grand Library of Snarks. But at least he was feeling like electricity again!

PLATFORM TEN

· THE SNARKSVILLE MARKET ·

To be honest, the Great Grand Library of Snarks was actually quite easy to find. (They probably didn't need a talking vacuum cleaner to lead the way.) You couldn't really miss it. It stood out on the hilltop horizon like an ENORMOUS honeycomb beehive; only it seemed to be made of paper, printed words and glass.

'It's magical!' Ella sighed with delight.

'It's one of Izzambard's nine hundred and ninety-eight wonders.' Cogg's sunroof flipped up with pride. 'And it's market day! We have to go through Snarksville to get to the library. Keep close, Warm Hearts from the Other World. Don't get lost.'

Ella grabbed one of Cogg's nozzles and they ran over the first little hill. Before them spread fields full of stalls with red and white canvas roofs. The smells wafting out of them were delicious. Not lavender, like on the railway platform. More like melted butter and honey. Some of the little stalls were selling hot pies and steaming dishes. Others, strange fruits and fairy dust. Leo couldn't help noticing that everyone was much taller than back home. Not only that. Their skin was lilac. And there were lots of beavers. Yes. How could I have forgotten to mention: there were a surprising number of beavers, standing upright

and serving whizzle-ade.

'Oh my!' shouted one, with particularly large teeth. 'They've smashed my pots again. And Mrs Brown's bonnets have been messed upon terribly!'

'What's the matter?' Ella asked, running over.

'Will you stop doing that!' Leo said, trying to catch up. 'You don't even know what these things are!'

'They are just beavers and purple people,' Ella said. 'And they look like they need our help!'

HUMMMMMMMMMMM said the Snarkifying Glass.

Ella turned to the beaver: 'Who has broken your pots and messed all over Mrs Brown's bonnets?'

'Griselda's heronites,' the beaver said. 'It's always heronites. Coming here, stealing our things for their nests and messing upon our treasures with their nasty oily poo. Especially on Snarskville Market Day.'

'Yuck!' Ella said.

'Heronites?' Leo repeated. 'What are they?'

The beaver looked confused.

'He's from the Other World,' Cogg explained. 'He doesn't understand much.'

Suddenly, one of the beavers pointed at the sky. In the distance, high above the clouds, there were flocks of tiny little 'V's, circling around the sun. Ella blinked. They glistened like mirrors and made her eyes hurt.

'Heronites,' a lilac man whispered. 'Griselda's mechanical birds. And they're coming closer.'

'And they don't just break pots,' said the beaver, clearing up the pieces from the stall. 'They try to destroy any scrap of Old Magic that is left. Our fairy dust. Our Flightly Wings. Our Forgotten Times powders and potions. The things that once made Snarksville great. They go back to the Time-Ticker's Palace to top up their oil levels, then return to destroy it all!'

'So why don't you stop them?' Leo asked.

'We've tried to stop them,' said the beaver. 'But Griselda just keeps making more.' There was a distant screech in the sky and the crowds ran in all directions. Some took cover beneath their stalls.

'Come on, Warm Hearts,' Cogg said. 'We need to hurry! When heronites are in the sky, Griselda is never far behind. We need to find the Chief Snarkarian.' They began to weave through the market place.

'Find the Chief Snarkarian,' a lilac lady with rather pointy ears said with a snort. 'I'd hardly her call her "Chief". Not these days. She's drowning in a sea of her own books. Don't see how she'll be able to help you.'

Cogg's middle-section swivelled: 'She will help us because Prince Bartholomew said she would. And Prince Bartholomew is always right.'

Suddenly, all the Snarkarians (and beavers that weren't yet hiding) bowed low: 'All hail to the Prince of Izzambard,' they said. (Ella and Leo stopped and bowed, too. Just to be on the safe side.)

'And now,' Cogg said, waving a nozzle aloft. 'We must find the Great Chief Snarkarian and help her. Before it's too late.'

HUMMMMMMMMMMM.

The beaver sniffed the air: 'WAIT! Is that what I think it is?'

'Probably,' Leo said.

All the beavers came out from under the stalls and sniffed the air, too. They began to gather round Leo. One of the tallest lilac ladies glided over. She held Leo's hand. 'This Warm Heart is in possession of the Snarkifying Glass. He may be able to save us all! For if the Great Grand Library of Snarks is in order, the Snarkarian will have more time and more magic to protect us, and the heronites will be afraid to come to our land.'

Leo blushed.

HUMMMMMMMMMMMM.

'Quick,' urged a large and bristly beaver, 'Take it to the Snarkarian!'

SCRREEEEEEEECHHHHHHH!

Ella screamed. An enormous bird had swept down from the skies and tried to grasp her bright red hat! Now, Ella could put up with many things. But she could NOT put up with something stealing her hat. Without even thinking, she grabbed the Snarkifying Glass and held it up to the sun. Then, she reflected a beam of burning sunlight onto the mechanical bird. It let out a terrible **SCRREEEECHHH** that echoed across the skies. Its wing glowed crimson as it spiralled toward the market and landed with a **CRAASHHHH** amongst some pots.

'Ella! What have you done?' gasped Leo. 'And where did you learn to do that?!'

'I don't know,' Ella said. She picked up her hat and brushed off the dust.

'We're in trouble now,' Cogg said, trying not to fall to pieces. But he couldn't help himself. A shiny metal bit fell off.

'Why?' Leo asked.

'Because the heronites are Griselda's spies. She'll know one is injured and he'll tell her that we're here. She'll send more to try to stop us returning the Snarkifying Glass. And then, the people of Snarksville will never be free. And Prince Barty will never be allowed to go home!'

'More heronites?'

Ella's lip began to tremble. 'Sorry, Leo. But . . . but . . . but . . . It was trying to take my red hat.'

There was another SCRREEEECH from the skies. This time, louder. And angrier. The flock of mechanical birds was descending!

'HIDE!' one of the beavers yelled, lifting a heavy white sheet that covered a stall.

Cogg, Leo, and Ella dived underneath the canvas so didn't see the incredible things that happened next. In fact, they couldn't see anything at all. They just blinked in the darkness.

'I don't like the dark,' Ella said.

'Quiet,' Leo whispered.

There were strange scratching noises and heavy wing beats brushing past the canvas.

SCRREEEEEEEECHHHHH!

More heronites, Leo thought. Then silence.

All Ella, Leo, and Cogg could hear was their own breath (and a slight suction). But then . . .

CLIPPETTY CLOP. CLIPPETTY CLOP.

It sounded like a horse. Getting closer and closer. Past their hiding place. It stopped! Ella held her breath. Cogg conked out.

CLIPPETTY CLOP. CLIPPETTY CLOP.

A swish of skirts along the floor. A powerful smell of wild garlic and mint.

CLIPPETTY CLOP. CLIPPETTY CLOP.

The silence was so loud it hurt your ears. Ella and Leo could hardly bear it. They both put their hands over theirs.

Suddenly, there was a single piercing **SCREEEEEEEECHHHHHHH** of rage.

'WHO DID THIS WICKEDNESS?' a woman's voice yelled. 'WHO DARED TO HURT ONE OF MY BIRDS?'

No answer. Just the hushed mutter of beavers and fear.

The horse neighed. Only, it didn't sound like a horse.

'You are right, we have no time for this,' the voice said . 'Or rather, they have no time . . . Destroy Snarksville.

I, Griselda, Master Clockmaker, demand it!'

CRASH. SMASH. SCREECH. CLATTER.

There were screams as beavers ran for cover. Cries as pots of fairy dust were thrown by beating wings to the ground. Then silence once again.

CLIPPETTY CLOP. CLIPPETTY CLOP. CLIPPETTY CLOP.

The sound of hooves faded into the distance: the soft slow rise of the crowds' voices, as the market returned to normal.

'You can come out now.' Three beavers' faces peered under the canvas. Ella and Leo stumbled out, Cogg following shakily behind. The heronites had gone. The horse had gone. But the market was a broken shell and only the smell of wild garlic and mint remained.

'What happened?' Ella asked.

Leo was too shocked to speak. He just held his little sister close to his side.

'It was the Clockmaker,' said the beaver. 'Astride her unicorn. We are safe now. But she will be back. She always comes back.'

'Quick,' the lilac lady with the ears said. 'You must leave this place. You must find the Chief Snarkarian. FAST!'

PLATFORM ELEVEN

· THE GREAT GRAND LIBRARY · OF SNARKS

Ella was good at a lot of things. Handstands. Skipping. Eating her vegetables. But she was not good at being fast.

'Wait for me!' she shouted.

Cogg was whizzing on ahead and Leo was already at the top of the hill, clambering up the stairs. 'How do we get in?' yelled Leo. 'I've found lots of hexagon windows. But I just can't find a door.'

'WHY WOULD A LIBRARY HAVE A DOOR?' Cogg shouted.

'So that you can get inside?' Leo said.

'Don't be silly. Libraries don't have doors.'

'Don't they?' Leo said.

'No. Of course not,' Cogg said.

'Then how do you get in?' Leo asked.

'Through the bottom.'

'Pardon?' Leo said.

'Through the bottom. Like bee hives. That's the best way of keeping books safe. Honestly. I thought Warm Hearts from the Other World were supposed to be clever.'

'We are clever,' Ella said, catching up.

Cogg made a funny noise (that isn't translatable into Warm Heart speak) and whizzed around the back of the Great Grand Library of Snarks. Ella and Leo chased after him, just in time to see him disappearing into a golden hexagon on the ground. Leo peered in. It seemed to twist deep beneath the earth. The Snarkifying Glass gently hummed.

'Leo. It looks a bit . . . very . . . dark,' Ella said.

Now, Ella LOVED most things. She loved fish fingers. She loved workshops. She loved butterflies. She loved trains. She loved Time Waders. She loved beavers. But she really, really, didn't like the DARK.

'Come on. It'll be OK,' Leo promised.

'No it won't,' Ella said. 'I'll wait outside.'

'You can't.'

'I can.'

'You can't. Griselda might find you.'

'I don't care.'

'Come on, Ella,' Leo said, stepping into the tunnel. 'We have to return the Snarkifying Glass. For Barty.'

HUMMMMMMMMMMMMMMM

'Not. Moving.' Ella folded her arms.

'Ella,' Leo said. 'The birds might try to steal your hat again.'

'My hat?' Ella paused. She loved her red hat. 'Really? Do you really think they will?'

'Definitely. That's definitely what they'd do. Mechanical birds are always stealing hats. Especially red ones.'

Ella touched her hat. She hated the dark. But she liked her hat **MORE** than she hated the dark. That meant that she would have to go in the tunnel! But it was very, very dark.

She stopped: 'Why can't Cogg take it back?'

'We agreed to this quest, Ella. We're the ones that found it. Come on. We need to give this back. Otherwise, we'll never get home!'

HUMMMMMMMM. The Snarkifying Glass agreed.

Ella took a deep breath, held onto her hat, and ran into her biggest fear.

PLATFORM TWELVE

·PETUNIA OLIVE·

Cogg was getting impatient. Time was ticking. (Unless Griselda had already stopped it.) And things kept landing on his sunroof! Umbrellas. Lollipops. Bicycles. Snowflakes. Curious objects falling off the shelves! Why were Ella and Leo taking so long? Where were they? Cogg was about to go back and find them, when they popped up into the light.

‘Whoa!’ Leo cried, a tiny spaceship whizzing past his nose. ‘This isn’t a library! It’s a . . . carnival!’

And it was! I mean, yes, there were books, mountains of books. But they weren’t neatly ordered on the shelves—they were everywhere; and the enormous hexagon-shaped hall was full of the strangest things Leo and Ella had ever seen! A flock of flamingos flamenco dancing, a man made of leaves with a hairdryer, a choir of caterpillars, and a witch whizzing about on her broom!

‘I LOVE LIBRARIES!’ Ella beamed.

‘No,’ Cogg said, pulling a lollipop out of his sun-roof. ‘Something is wrong. It's not supposed to be like this. The Chief Snarkarian normally has everything under control. Where is she? Where's Petunia Olive?'

'Help!' a tiny, muffled voice cried. It was coming from beneath a pile of books.

'Petunia? Petunia Olive? Is that you?' Cogg said.

'Help,' the voice said again.

Still being showered by lollipops, Leo ran over and started digging his way through the books. There, at the bottom, was a rosy-cheeked woman with a pair of broken spectacles hanging off her nose.

'Well, thank goodness for that, my dearypops!' she said, letting Leo

heave her up. 'To be thinking, I was drowning in a sea of my own books! Without my Snarkarian Magnifying Glass, I can't be a'keeping them in order, you see. And everything is getting out of hand! Oh! Look! My poor library. The books won't stay in place. I can't even findle the rightative shelves. And when I don't findle the rightative shelves, well, you can see for yourselfums!'

A tiny hippopotamouse flew past Ella's ear. (Please note: this is not a misspelling. It was NOT a hippopotamus. It was a hippopotamouse. They are completely different things.)

'Good gracious, my dearypops,'

Petunia said. 'What an awfulosity! The characters from the Snarkarian book collection are getting quite wilderacious.'

'Wow!' gasped Ella.

'Well, it may be very excitabilitive. But it's not at all proper or fine!'

HUMMMMMMMMMMMMMM

'Wait! Is that? Is that? Is that what I thinkle it is?' Petunia grabbed Leo's arm. Very carefully, he pulled the griffin-trimmed Snarkifying Glass out of his pocket.

HUMMMMMMMMMMMMMM

'Oh my. Such joyiosity! The Snarkifying Glass is back! Back in the rightful hand of a Snarkarian. May I?' She took it from Leo's hand. 'I never thought I'd be seeing again the day. Back where it is of belonging. Now, with the help of this wonderfluss Snarkifier, I'll be able to put everything in place. Oh, my dearypops. You are all so true and kind.'

'Would you like some help?' asked Leo, who had not forgotten his Other World manners.

'Oh, yes please my dearypops,' Petunia said. Ella tried not to giggle. She was the funniest Snarkarian Ella had ever met. Well. She was the only

Snarkarian Ella had ever met. But you know what I mean. Petunia leapt about, Snarkifying Glass in hand, putting the books back on the proper shelves.

'Use the ladder-ups, my wonderlies. No time to us can be lost.'

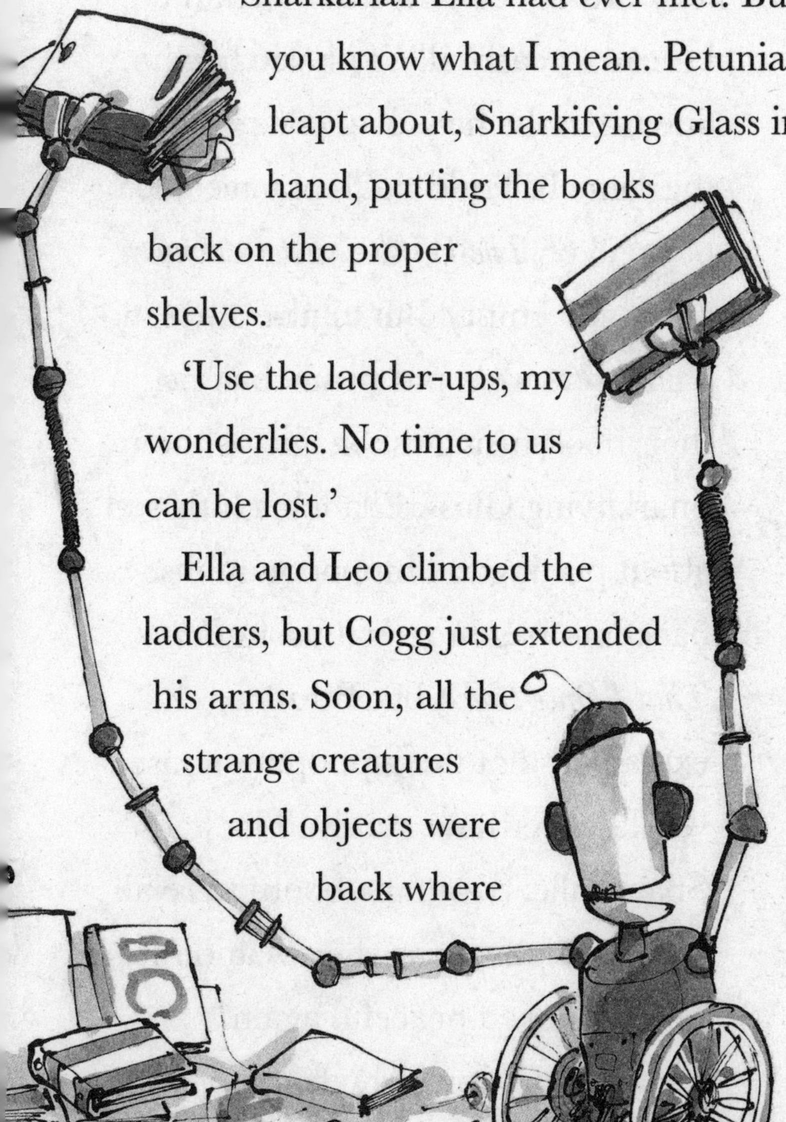

Ella and Leo climbed the ladders, but Cogg just extended his arms. Soon, all the strange creatures and objects were back where they belonged. And when I say 'all', I mean, 'nearly all'. The witch (who, one can only guess had escaped out of the tunnel), could not be found—so page 38 of *The Witches in the Chimney* remained empty. But all the other characters were put neatly back in their books using the magic of the Snarkifying Glass. Ella felt a little sad about putting the hippopotamouse back into page 104 of *Curious Beasts That I Once Knew*, but Petunia explained that the hippopotamouse would never have survived in Snarksville. Soon, the books were all stacked high on the shelves and the library looked peaceful again.

'Now, my wonderly dearypops,'

Petunia said, stroking the Snarkifying Glass and collapsing onto a chair. 'What can I do for you diddlies in return?'

'We need to get back to the Other World,' Leo said.

'Other World?' Petunia repeated. 'But I thought all the doors had been locked. Handles all thrown into yonderly.'

'They have. That's why they need the Sleeping Key,' Cogg explained. 'And we must be quick! Prince Barty is waiting for them on the platform.'

'Oh my! The Princeypops. We mustn't keep him a'waiting. I've read what'll happen to him if we do. Vines. Them's is terrible vines. And to stay on a train for ever. There's nothing of the likes that can be worse!'

'So, can we have the Sleeping Key?' Leo asked.

'In all my heart, I would love nothing better than to have been giving it you, Other Worldly wonderlies. What an honour. But I'm afraid that the Sleeping Key is gone!'

'Where?'

'Of that mysterosity, I do not know.'

'You mean we're stuck! In Izzambard?' Leo cried.

Suddenly, they heard screeching from outside the library.

'It be the squawking heronites, what is sent from Griselda,' Petunia said. 'I'll come outside and fight them off with the powers of my Snarkifying Glass. Snarksville will be wonderfluss again, now I've got more time and magic, thanks to you diddlies. But you must be's a'running.'

'But we still don't have the key!'

'That be true, my wonderlies. But I have read and seen what you have not. You must go before the vines start to creep. Otherwise, the Kingdom of Izzambard will be lost. Good Luck!'

What could Ella and Leo do? They had no choice. They left the library and ran back to the platform as fast as they could. The skies all an echo with **SCREEEEEEEEEEECHHHHH!!!!**

PLATFORM THIRTEEN

· THE MECHANICAL BIRDS ·

Being chased by a flock of mechanical birds is one of the worst things that can ever happen to you. Trust me. It really is. And right now, Leo, Ella, and Cogg were having one of the worst times of their lives.

'QUICK!' Leo shouted, sprinting along the side of the railway track. The train was puffing out steam at the other end of the track.

'But they're everywhere,' Ella cried, holding tightly onto her hat.

And they were! Hundreds of them! Huge, mechanical heronites with silver wings beating against the sky.

'Leo. Cogg. Wait. I can't run any more. I'm all out of puff.'

'You've got to!' Leo yelled.

'Run, Ella. Do it for the Prince,' Cogg cried.

'But I can't.'

Suddenly, one of the birds broke away from the flock and swooped down towards Ella. It had one very scorched-looking wing and outstretched talons. It was the bird that Ella had zapped with the Snarkifying Glass. She was sure of it.

'Ella! Get down!' Leo screamed.

But Ella didn't 'get down'.

(It's hard to 'get down' when an enormous mechanical bird is flying straight towards your head.) Ella gulped and carried on looking up.

Leo knew this was a 'big brother' moment. He ran towards Ella as if she was a rugby ball and threw himself on top.

'OOOooof!' Ella said.

'SQUUUUUARK!' cried the bird, as it whizzed past and crashed into the trees.

CRASH! THWUNK! KERPLING!

The bird's huge metal wings crumpled against the bark and springs and screws dropped onto the grass. For a second, everything went quiet. Even the beating of wings in the sky. Leo looked up. As if controlled by something from afar, all the birds had started gliding upwards and swung back behind the clouds and flew away!

'Ufff.' Leo could hear Ella's

muffled voice beneath him but he didn't move an inch. Not yet. Ella pushed her way out, all pink-faced and hot.

'H . . . have they gone?' Ella asked, wriggling out from beneath her brother.

'Yes,' Leo whispered. 'They've gone. They must have run out of oil or been scared away by Petunia Olive. Are you OK?'

'No,' Ella cried, getting up. 'My lovely hat is all squashed!' She picked it up from the ground.

Cogg gently vacuumed her back.

'Forget the hat! Are you OK?' Leo asked.

'I think so.' Ella dusted her hat off

and jammed it back on her head. 'But what about the bird, Leo? Is it dead?'

'I don't think it was ever alive,' Leo said.

'Of course it was alive, Leo. All of Griselda's clockwork things are alive! Cogg is clockwork and he's the Prince's best friend.'

'But I am half Warm Heart,' Cogg pointed out.

CHOOOOOOOO CHOOOOOOOOO
HISSSSSSSSSSSSSSSSS

'Hurry! Let's get to the train before the vines come!' Leo said. It was standing on the platform in a cloud of butterflies and steam.

The three of them ran

towards the train as fast as they could and leapt onto the back of the engine. Lord and Lady Asquith twitched and began shovelling coal into the engine.

CHOOOOOOOO CHOOOOOOOOO!

'Oh, thank goodness you're back!' Barty cried, running into the engine and wiping his forehead with his hankie. 'The vines are creaking and I thought we might have run out of time!'

'We just saw—' Leo began.

'WATCH OUT!' Barty shouted. 'G . . . G . . . Griselda's vines!' The metal leaves were beginning to crawl across the platform.

'Don't let them steal my hat!' Ella yelled.

'Shovel, dear Asquiths,' Barty shouted.

'It's no good.' Leo pulled a vine off a window. 'We'll never get away in time.'

'Yes, we will,' Barty insisted. 'Lord Asquith had the most brilliant idea whilst you were in Snarksville. But we can only use it once!'

Lord Asquith took a little bow.

'Hold onto your hat.' Barty pulled a twisting vine off his shoulder and yanked a metal lever hard.

PLATFORM FOURTEEN

· BUSHY-TAILED TURBO POWER ·

The train FLEW through the air. Well, actually, I'm not going to lie to you. The train didn't fly through the air. But it did WHIZZZ at an incredible speed. Sparks flew and the engine roared. And you know how your cheeks go when you're on a rollercoaster? Well, Leo's and Ella's cheeks went like that.

'Euuu gaaaa maaa ooooo,' Ella said.

'Hooo aull wa,' Leo said.

(It's hard to talk when your cheeks are pulled right back and I've absolutely no idea what they said.) Snarksville Platform disappeared in a flash, and whatever was outside the windows was a blur: they were going far too fast to see. Finally, the train began to slow down. The station where they began was just up ahead!

'How marvellous! How absolutely wonderful!' Barty said, clapping his hands in delight. 'It worked! We escaped. We're back to Platform One. Lord Asquith, you are a genius.'

Lord Asquith blushed as much as your average genius waistcoated squirrel can. Lady Asquith looked less happy.

'Sorry, Lady Asquith. You were a triumph. Dear Lady Asquith, please have a rest. Cogg will bring you some whizzle-ade! Cogg. Go and get the trolley.'

Lady Asquith did look a little faint. (The only problem with Lord Asquith's turbo-boost invention was that Lady Asquith had to shovel seventeen times as fast. This is not good for a squirrel.

That's why they could only use the booster once.)

'Look, Leo!' Ella was pointing out the window. 'I can see our station! With the stone platform and the glistening vines.'

'Griselda's glistening vines, you mean!' Leo said. 'They don't look so nice now!' Leo was rubbing his cheeks to see if they were back to normal. As he did so, his thoughts went back to normal, too.

'Barty!' he said, angrily. 'We did as you said. We returned the Snarkarian's Snarkifying Glass. But Petunia Olive DIDN'T have the Sleeping Key! You told us she had it! You told us she'd help us get back home.'

'Ah, yes, about that,' said Barty. He lifted his cap and took something out. Something key shaped. Something asleep. Something key shaped and asleep! THE SLEEPING KEY!!

'What? You mean you had it all the time? You tricked us!' Leo yelled.

'Well, the thing is . . . yes . . . I'm sorry about that.'

Cogg started vacuuming Leo's back to calm him down but the Sleeping Key just yawned.

'How could you? How could you trick us? I thought you were supposed to be our friend!'

'I am your friend,' Barty said.

'Friends don't tell lies,' Ella said, holding Leo's hand.

'And we got attacked by mechanical birds! And nearly caught by Griselda at the market! And we nearly got crushed by Griselda's vines! We've risked our lives for you!'

'Yes. And we risked my red hat,' Ella said.

'Call yourself a prince?' Leo said. 'You're no prince at all!'

Barty blushed. Then, Barty gulped: 'I'm terribly sorry,' he said. 'But I needed you to return the Snarkifying Glass. It's the only way to help Izzambard. If you'd known the Sleeping Key was under my cap all the time, you wouldn't have done it.'

'Yes, we would,' Ella said.

Barty looked at Leo. Leo sighed.

'No, we wouldn't,' he said. 'I'd have grabbed the key and got us back home. But still, it's horrible to tell lies, Barty. It makes everything shaky. Especially friendship. You must promise never to do it again!'

'I promise. And I'm so sorry,' said the Prince. 'Here. Take it. It's yours.' He held out the key.

'Please stop vacuuming my back,' Leo said. Cogg stopped. 'Now, tell me. How does the Sleeping Key work?'

'Just whisper to it. Tell it what you want. It will help you open any handle-less door. But don't lose it. It's very special. It's . . . ' He lowered his voice: 'Old Magic. From since the time that Buckle Rule began. And it's the only way a Warm Heart can get out of Izzambard.'

Very carefully, Leo took the key from Barty's hands. It yawned again.

Ella giggled.

'I LOVE sleeping keys,' she said.

The train was barely moving now. Time seemed to be slowing down. Leo wondered if that was Griselda's doing. Was she playing with something clockwork somewhere?

'As soon as you're back in the Other World,' Barty said, 'let the key go back to sleep. Sleeping keys can't stay awake long. If they do, well, things start to go wrong.'

'OK.' Leo put it in his pocket. He could feel its breath on his leg!

The train stopped. 'You'd best go. Quickly,' Barty said. 'But please promise to come back. There're more magical objects to find. And

G . . . G . . . G . . .'

'We know,' Leo said.

'And we promise,' Ella said.

'Do Warm Hearts from the Other World always tell the truth?' asked Barty.

'Yes,' Leo said.

'No,' Ella said.

Cogg and Barty looked confused.

'Warm Hearts from the Other World tell lies quite a lot, but we won't,' Ella said.

'No. We won't,' Leo added. 'We'll be back.'

'Because you don't like things being shaky?' Cogg said.

'That's right.' Leo grinned.

'Marvellous.' Barty beamed and

patted the top of Ella's red hat. Ella kissed Barty, and Leo shook his hand. Cogg vacuumed them both lightly on the back. Then, they jumped onto the platform. Suddenly, there was a huge gush of steam and tiny butterflies. Leo and Ella couldn't see the train at all.

'DON'T FORGET THE KINGDOM OF IZZAMBARD,' Barty boomed. 'ITS FUTURE LIES IN YOUR HANDS.'

· RETURN TICKETS PLEASE! ·

Leo and Ella ran as fast as they could past Griselda's glistening vines, just hoping that they didn't start to creak.

'How can I put a key in something that doesn't have a lock?' Leo asked, rubbing his hands against the handle-less door.

'Just try,' Ella said. 'Get the Sleeping Key out! And tell it what you want.'

So Leo did. He whispered very gently: 'Home, please.' He felt a bit silly because it looked like any ordinary metal key. Only it wriggled a little. And then it yawned. And then (and this is quite strange), it sniffed!

'It can smell something,' Ella said. The key made a little cough.

'It's coughing,' Leo said, trying not to drop it.

'Look!' Ella and Leo watched in amazement as a keyhole appeared in the door. The key sniffed again. (Well, more of a snort, actually.)

'Put it in! Put it in!' Ella said, jumping up and down.

Leo put the key into the just-appeared keyhole and turned it hard. It opened with a **CLICK**. Leo and Ella didn't wait. They pushed the door and fell into THE OTHER WORLD (or This World, depending how you look at it) with a **BUMP**.

'It's the workshop!' Leo grinned. 'We're back!'

The Sleeping Key yawned and stretched. 'Put it away! Quick!' Ella said, 'Before things start to go wrong!'

Leo tucked the key into his pocket once again.

Now, I could tell you all about the strange and curious objects that were hidden in the workshop, shimmering beneath the dust. But the objects weren't ready to be found yet and the red circles on the timetable weren't even twitching.

Leo and Ella were desperate to get back home and so they ran through the wood as fast as they could and charged into the kitchen at the Station House.

'Mum! Dad! We missed you,' Leo said, throwing himself into Mrs Leggit's arms. (He hadn't done this since he was little so Mrs Leggit was a little concerned.) 'Are you all right?' she asked, pulling Leo off. 'You've only been gone a little while.'

'Yes. Of course I am. I'm just glad to see you again. That's all.'

'Me too!' Ella said, hurling herself at Mr Leggit.

'If you want sweets, you're not getting any,' Mr Leggit said. 'Not until Friday. Remember what the dentist said.'

'We don't want sweets,' Leo said. 'We're just happy to be home.'

Ella beamed.

'Hmmmmm,' Mr Leggit said,

sounding just like the Snarkifying Glass. He emptied another box.

'You're wearing a hat,' Mrs Leggit said.

'Isn't it beautiful?' Ella replied. 'It nearly got stolen by Griselda's mechanical birds. And snatched by the Evil Clockmaker's vines. And if we hadn't taken the Snarkifying Glass back to the Snarkarian, the last little bits of Old Magic would have all been covered in heronite mess and completely destroyed!'

'Of course they would, darling.' Mrs Leggit smiled. 'Two fish fingers or three?'

'Three, please.' Leo sighed. 'Trying to save the Prince and stopping Griselda from harming the Kingdom of Izzambard is hungry work.'

Mr Leggit blinked.

Mrs Leggit called Mr Leggit over to the pantry. 'Don't worry, Hugo,' she whispered. 'They're just overexcited. It's probably the move. Just go along with it.'

'Right ho.' Mr Leggit tapped his nose. He turned to face Leo and Ella. 'As long as you're happy, children, that's the main thing. Are you happy? Do you like your new house?'

'Yes,' Leo said.

'We love it,' Ella agreed.

'So you don't think the Station House is dull?'

'Dull? No! It's the most exciting place I've ever lived in and I want to stay here for ever,' Ella said.

'And the Kingdom of Izzambard needs us,' Leo added. Ella put her little hand in his and squeezed hard. To be honest, he'd never felt more like electricity.

Mr Leggit looked at Mrs Leggit. 'Isn't it lovely? To see them getting on so well.'

'It's the move, dear,' was all Mrs Leggit managed to say.

Leo and Ella gobbled down their

fish fingers and had a hot bath before bed. They didn't put up the usual bedtime struggle. They didn't moan about wanting to stay up late. They didn't even mind about sleeping head to toe in the same room. (Mr Leggit had only assembled one bed.) They were both absolutely exhausted!

'Good night,' Mr Leggit and Mrs Leggit said, kissing them both on the cheeks.

'Good night,' Leo said.

'Good night,' Ella said.

'Yawn,' said the Sleeping Key.

ALL ABOARD

for an **EXCLUSIVE** extract of:

due to arrive in **JULY 2016**!

'THE TRAIN NOW ARRIVING AT PLATFORM ONE IS THE 11:61 IZZAMBARD EXPRESS. STOPPING AT SNARKSVILLE, THE CRYSTAL CAVES, THE—' The voice suddenly stopped. Barty leapt into the carriage.

'Gosh! You were quick!' said Barty, wiping his forehead with his hankie and hugging them both. 'Well done! Bravo! Come along! Jump on board!' Cogg lightly vacuumed Leo's cheek. Leo tried his very best not to mind.

'But we weren't quick,' said Ella, squeezing Barty tight. 'We've been *ages*.'

'Weeks, in fact,' chimed in Leo, pulling Cogg's nozzle off his back. 'We thought you'd be worried. In trouble, perhaps?'

'Trouble? We've barely had time to wash our socks.'

'I don't wear socks,' said Cogg.

'Nor do I,' said Barty, wriggling his toes. 'But I'm trying to speak "Other World". Anyway, I know what must have happened. Other World time stops when you come here. But our time stops when you go home. I think. Unless Griselda's been playing about with time in Izzambard again? Oh dear. Maybe that's it? One never really knows.'

'It doesn't matter,' Ella said. 'I don't understand time anyway, even when it does what it's *supposed* to. But I do understand hammers. Look! It's full of light.' She shone her little hammer necklace at them all.

Barty gasped: 'Well, blow me down and call me a will-o'-the-wisp! It's the Incredible Crystallator!'

Leo blinked. 'The what?'

'Incredible Crystallator,' Ella said, beaming at the hammer with pride.

'Is it dangerous?' Leo asked.

'No. Well, not in the right hands.' Barty adjusted his cap and looked thoughtful.

'Are my hands the right hands?' Ella asked, looking at her fingers.

'Definitely,' Barty smiled. 'But the Incredible Crystallator would be dangerous in Griselda's. That's all I meant. It should be in the hand of Gripendulum, the High Chief Goblin of the Crystal Caves.'

'He must be very small,' said Leo.

'Of course he's not "very small".

He's the leader of the Hobgoblins.'

'Well, his hammer is very small.' Leo looked at the shining object dangling around Ella's neck. A tiny blue clockwork butterfly fluttered past.

'Shhh! Griselda's spies!' Barty leant closer and whispered: 'Things aren't always what they seem, Leo. This is Izzambard, remember.' Barty's voice rose to a normal pitch. 'Cogg. Would you be so kind as to debutterfly the carriage?'

'Of course, Your Highness.' Cogg swivelled a nozzle and blew out a huge stream of blue air. The butterfly clattered to the floor. Then, it flew away. 'Debutterflying complete,' said Cogg. But Barty had disappeared.

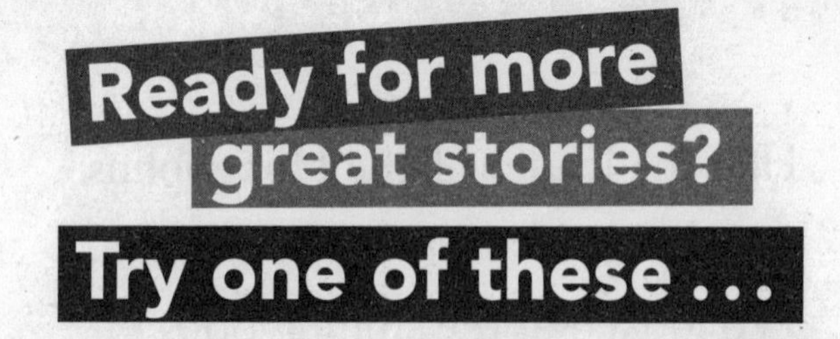
Ready for more
great stories?
Try one of these . . .

Unicorn in New York
LOUIE LETS LOOSE!
It's time for this unicorn to shine!
I ♥ NY
RACHEL HAMILTON
Illustrated by
OSCAR ARMELLES
SOMETHING'S OUT OF CONTROL IN THE CLASSROOM . . .
AND FOR ONCE IT ISN'T THE KIDS
CREATURE TEACHER
SCIENCE SHOCKER
SAM WATKINS and ILLUSTRATED BY David O'Connell
Nelly and the Quest for Captain Peabody
ONE GIRL.
ONE TURTLE.
ONE EPIC VOYAGE.
ROLAND CHAMBERS
ILLUSTRATED BY ELLA OKSTAD
PUGS OF THE FROZEN NORTH
BY PHILIP REEVE
AND
SARAH MCINTYRE